Snap books™

Girls Got Game

girls'
FIGURE SKATING
Ruling the Rink

by Heather E. Schwartz

Consultant
Mary-Elizabeth Wightman
U.S. Figure Skating Judge

Capstone
press®
Mankato, Minnesota

Snap Books are published by Capstone Press,
151 Good Counsel Drive, P.O. Box 669, Mankato, Minnesota 56002.
www.capstonepress.com

Library of Congress Cataloging-in-Publication Data

Schwartz, Heather E.
  Girls' figure skating: ruling the rink / by Heather E. Schwartz.
    p. cm.—(Snap books. Girls got game)
  Summary: "Describes figure skating, the skills needed for it, and ways
to compete"—Provided by publisher.
  Includes bibliographical references and index.
  ISBN-13: 978-0-7368-6822-8 (hardcover)
  ISBN-10: 0-7368-6822-4 (hardcover)
  1. Figure skating for girls. I. Title. II. Series.
GV850.4.S38 2007
796.91'2—dc22   2006021249

Editor: Amber Bannerman

Designer: Bobbi J. Wyss

Photo Researcher: Charlene Deyle

Photo Credits: Capstone Press/Karon Dubke, 16, 19, 20, 21, 25; Capstone Press/TJ Thoraldson Digital Photography,
12, 14, 15, 18, 24; Comstock Klips, back cover; Corbis/Bohemian Nomad Picturemakers, 9; Corbis/David Bergman, cover;
Corbis/For Picture/Stephane Reix, 6; Corbis/Patrik Giardino, 7; Corbis/Wally McNamee, 5; Corbis/ZUMA/SDU-T/K.C.
Alfred, 26; Getty Images Inc./AFP/Jacques Demarthon, 28; Getty Images Inc./AFP/John MacDougall, 11; Getty Images
Inc./Bongarts/Vladimir Rys, 29; Getty Images Inc./Hulton Archive, 8; Getty Images Inc./Robert Laberge, 13, 22-23;
Getty Images Inc./Stuart Franklin, 27; Hot Shots Photo, 32; Synchronized Skating Magazine, 17

Acknowledgements:
Capstone Press would like to thank Karen Cover from the World Figure Skatng Museum and Hall of Fame in Colorado
Springs, Colorado, for help in reviewing this book.

Capstone Press would like to thank the *Hockettes* for supplying the photo of synchronized skating.

1 2 3 4 5 6 12 11 10 09 08 07

TABLE OF CONTENTS

CHAPTER ONE

CAN'T WAIT TO SKATE

Have you ever watched figure skaters on TV and thought, "I want to do that"? Jumping, spinning, gliding gracefully—superstar skaters like Michelle Kwan and Kimmie Meissner make it all look so easy. You'd hardly guess they even had to practice. Then you try some of those moves and—surprise! It turns out they're not so simple at all. Still, there's no reason you can't learn to skate like a pro. In fact, you probably already have some of the skills you need to succeed.

Do you like to play sports? Sing and dance? If so, you'll fit right in on the ice, where muscles, stamina, and lots of creative energy are required. Skaters are athletes, but they're also artists. They design original routines to impress judges, entertain a crowd, and showcase their hard work.

Do you have what it takes? Sure you do! The pros didn't start at the top. They began with hopes, dreams, and plans, just like you. All you have to do is take that first step.

Michelle
Kwan

Can You Compete?

Figure skating is a sport that takes lots of hard work and dedication. First things first— you need to learn how to skate. Take lessons, or have a friend or relative who knows how to skate help you learn how. Practice at a skating club or at a recreational skating rink. In no time, you'll be ready to show off your skills.

Competitive figure skaters take tests, perform for judges, and challenge themselves against other skaters. With a lot of hard work, they even have the chance to make it to the Olympics. If you love the rush of a great competition, figure skating could be the sport for you.

Skills and Strength

If you've ever danced ballet or skied, you'll have an edge on the ice. Both activities use many of the same skills and muscles needed for figure skating. Balance, good posture, and strong, powerful legs are key to figure skating.

Join the Champs

If your ankles wobble, who cares? Get out on the ice. You'll join a strong tradition of girls and women who found success on skates. And it wasn't easy for them either. When Norwegian Sonja Henie skated in the 1924 Olympics, she had to stop several times to consult her coach. She earned last place that time, but returned to win gold medals in 1928, 1932, and 1936.

American skater Tenley Albright overcame childhood polio to win an Olympic gold in 1956. And did Dorothy Hamill let a little thing like not owning figure skates keep her off the ice? No way. She learned on her brother's hockey skates, stuffing the toes with socks to make them fit. Her reward? An Olympic gold medal in 1976.

Sonja Henie

Dorothy Hamill

" I wasn't particularly athletic or gifted, but I loved it. I'd be at the skating rink all day long, just skating around and around. "
—Dorothy Hamill

CHAPTER TWO

SKATING BY THE RULES

What makes skating a sport anyway? Good question. There's a big difference between figure skating and recreational skating, where everybody skates in a big circle.

In the sport of figure skating, skaters tackle difficult movements like jumps and spins. They practice for hours to get movements just right. Figure skaters create routines set to music and perform in shows and competitions. As a figure skater, you get to use all the ice, not just the narrow, crowded path around the edge of the rink.

Miki Ando

"Gold is the color of champions. I wanted to be the champion so I changed to gold."
—Miki Ando, talking about wearing gold blades on her skates during the 2004 World Junior Figure Skating Championships, where she won the gold medal.

How to Play

Figure skating is a competitive sport, but you don't really "play" it. How does it work? Most girls start out as singles skaters, meaning they skate alone. Before they can compete, they test to determine their level of ability. That way, they can be sure they're skating against other skaters with similar skills.

Now, Don't Get Testy

Figure skating tests aren't much like exams in school. Instead, you'll hit the ice to demonstrate your skating skills. Rather than aiming for an "A," you'll work toward a "pass" from judges. Then you're ranked and ready to compete.

CHAPTER THREE

GETTING STARTED

Becoming a great figure skater is a bit like building a house. You don't build the attic first, right? You start with a foundation and work up to the top floors. In figure skating, basic skills are your foundation. You build on them and learn harder moves when you're ready. You'll learn these basics in beginner classes.

Forward skating
A diagonal motion called stroking helps you push off and gain speed.

Crossovers
You'll cross one foot over the other while skating forward and backward.

Backward skating
The swizzle method involves moving feet
from toes together to heels together.

Turns
You'll need to know how to turn forward
to backward and backward to forward.

Proper posture
Look up and position arms slightly
out to the sides for balance.

Beyond the Basics

Practice will help perfect your skating skills. Local skating clubs can help you advance, whether you want to compete or skate in ice shows. Find a club through a skating rink or search online.

The private attention one-on-one lessons can give you may be just what you need. Many figure skating coaches teach group lessons and also take on private students.

Synchronized Skating

Wish you could skate with a partner or team? Now's your chance. Your club or coach can help you find a partner or a team and get started. Pairs skating features lifts and jumps and looks like two skaters moving as one. Ice dancing can be done with a partner or alone. This discipline focuses on rhythm and precise steps and may remind you of ballroom dancing. Synchronized skating requires skaters to move in unison. Teams are judged on things like originality, footwork, and speed.

CHAPTER FOUR

BECOMING THE BEST

Skating levels work almost like grades in school. As you learn new things and take tests to prove your skills, you move to the next level. Then you can compete against more advanced skaters. How fast you move forward depends on how much you practice, but many figure skaters spend about a year at each level. The tests and levels set by U.S. Figure Skating take skaters all the way to the Olympics. Pass the first one, and you're on your way.

The Fun Stuff

Before each test, you get to create your own routine set to music. You can even pick out a cool skating costume to wear. Costumes are sold through catalogs and at skating competitions. Some girls design their own costumes.

You don't have to dress up too much for a test. A practice dress or borrowed costume will do just fine. The important thing is to plan a routine that includes the specific required moves for your level. And don't be afraid to have fun—judges don't expect perfection from beginners.

Figure Skating Levels

Singles skaters test in a category called free skating. A skater passes from level to level by performing in a test session in front of three judges.

If the majority of the judges pass a skater, the skater moves to the next level. If the skater doesn't pass, she can retake the test in 28 days.

One-foot Spin

Spiral

Pre-preliminary

Start here with the basics, as well as moves like a waltz jump and a one-foot spin. When you pass, move ahead to the preliminary level.

Preliminary

This level requires many of the same moves you did in your first test—with more power and confidence. Spend some time here, then try to advance to the pre-juvenile level.

Sit-spin

Layback Spin

Juvenile

Here, you'll add an axel jump to your routine. Movements should match the music and use all the ice. Work hard, then try to advance to the intermediate level.

Axel

Pre-juvenile

Judges get pickier and want to see good posture, power, and flow in your movements. Keep practicing, then try for the juvenile level.

Intermediate

Show off all the skills that got you this far. Your skating should look powerful, precise, and effortless.

Ready for the Big Time?

Figure skaters who've passed their juvenile and intermediate tests get to compete in regional competitions. The top four skaters from each regional competition go on to compete in Junior Nationals.

For a shot at the Olympics, you'll need to pass tests that take you beyond the intermediate level to become a novice, junior, then senior level skater. At these levels, skaters also go to regional competitions—there are nine held throughout the country.

At each regional competition, skaters perform in one of four categories: ladies' singles, men's singles, pairs, or ice dancing. The top skaters from each category go on to sectional competitions. There are three sectionals throughout the country. At each, the whole process repeats itself and the top four skaters are selected for U.S. National Championships. From there, skaters are selected for international and world competitions. Only the top two or three skaters qualify for the Olympics.

Shizuka Arakawa, 2006 Olympics

23

Practice Makes Perfect

No matter what your skating level, you'll improve with practice. Keep getting out on the ice. But don't go out there cold. Serious skaters warm up their muscles first by jogging in place, jumping rope, or doing jumping jacks until they break a sweat.

Cooling down is important too, and you can do the same exercises when practice is over. Ask your coach for more ideas. Your coach should have some good advice when it comes to exercises that will help your performance.

Work Those Muscles

Off-ice conditioning will prepare you for on-ice training. Build up your strength and work on your balance. You'll not only perform better on skates, but you'll also avoid injury.

Push-ups, abdominal curls, and squats will strengthen your skating muscles. Practice these and in no time you'll be skating faster, jumping higher, and sticking those landings.

PRO PLAYERS

You've seen them dazzle crowds and win Olympic medals. These girls are today's figure skating stars. They're amazingly talented. They're also living proof that hard work and dedication can really pay off.

When Kimmie Meissner was 6, she spent a lot of time watching her older brothers skate and play hockey. Meissner grew up to skate her way to the 2006 Winter Olympics when she was 16. She finished sixth, then went on to win the World Championship. Meissner's motto: "Enjoy what you do, do what you enjoy."

Kimmie Meissner

Michelle Kwan

The most decorated figure skater in U.S. history, Michelle Kwan began skating at age 5 and won her first competition when she was 7. Since then, she's won 42 championships and two Olympic medals—a silver in 1998 and a bronze in 2002.

What's that pendant hanging around her neck when she skates? It's a Chinese good luck charm from her grandmother. She may have had some luck, but Kwan worked hard to perfect her skating. Her daily schedule included three 45-minute sessions on the ice, plus she spent another hour at the gym and ran $3\frac{1}{2}$ miles (5.6 kilometers) every day to stay in shape.

Irina Slutskaya

Russian skater Irina Slutskaya is best known for her trademark triple Lutz-triple loop combination. This element has helped her win several medals throughout the years. In 1996, Slutskaya was the first Russian woman to win the European Championships. At the 2002 Olympics, Slutskaya won a silver medal. In 2003, she faced health problems that forced her to take a break from skating. Today, she takes medication for her symptoms and is able to skate again.

Her health struggles have made her even more aware of what she loves in life—skating. Slutskaya went on to win a bronze medal at the 2006 Olympics. She hopes to inspire people "to have faith that you can find your way out of anything."

On ice, Japanese skater Shizuka Arakawa trains for $2\frac{1}{2}$ hours a day, six days a week. She also makes time for fitness when she's not skating. That hard work, along with skating since the age of 5, helped Arakawa win a gold medal at the 2006 Olympics. Besides skating, Arakawa enjoys listening to music, cooking, reading, and traveling.

Shizuka Arakawa

Could your name join this list one day? Just keep learning, practicing, and skating your best. You'll be amazed at what you can do!

GLOSSARY

axel (ACK-sil)—a jump in which the skater skates forward, turns one and a half times or more in the air, and then lands and skates backward

choreography (kor-ee-OG-ruh-fee)—the arrangement of dance steps and movements for a show

Lutz (LUTS)—a jump in which a skater glides backward in a wide curve and uses her toe pick to launch and rotate in the opposite direction

Salchow (SAL-kow)—a jump that starts from the back inside edge of the blade on one foot and lands on the back outside edge of the blade on the other foot

swizzle (SWI-zil)—an in-and-out movement on inside edges of skate that gets you going forward or backward

FAST FACTS

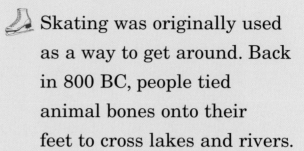

Skating was originally used as a way to get around. Back in 800 BC, people tied animal bones onto their feet to cross lakes and rivers.

Jackson Haines invented modern figure skating in the 1860s. Back then, Americans weren't crazy about his ideas, which combined skating with music and ballet dancing. But when he brought the new sport to Vienna, people there loved it. Figure skating became popular in the United States in 1914, the year the U.S. National Championships began.

READ MORE

Feldman, Jane. *I Am a Skater.*
Young Dreamers. New York: Random
House, 2002.

Jones, Jen. *Figure Skating for Fun!*
For Fun! Minneapolis: Compass Point
Books, 2006.

Peterson, Todd. *Michelle Kwan: Figure
Skater.* Ferguson Career Biographies.
New York: Ferguson, 2006.

INTERNET SITES

FactHound offers a safe, fun way to
find Internet sites related to this book.
All of the sites on FactHound have been
researched by our staff.

Here's how:

1. Visit *www.facthound.com*

2. Choose your grade level.

3. Type in this book ID **0736868224** for
   age-appropriate sites. You may also
   browse subjects by clicking on letters,
   or by clicking on pictures and words.

4. Click on the **Fetch It** button.

**Facthound will fetch the best sites
for you!**

ABOUT THE AUTHOR

Heather E. Schwartz has always loved writing, especially for kid-friendly publications like *Girls' Life, Guideposts for Kids,* and *Teen*. She started getting interested in sports writing when she interviewed Olympic swimmer Amy Van Dyken and golf great Annika Sorenstam. Heather was not much of an ice skater until she started writing this book. In order to make sure her research was spot-on, she took lessons and found herself learning to stroke forward, swizzle backward, and even do the crossover. Heather hopes readers will feel as inspired as she did to find success on the ice.

INDEX